A Red Chicken Named Blue

A story of forgiveness

Dedicated to my boys,
May your dreams become your richest realities. You can do anything.

Illustrations for O-Z-J-D-J-L-N,
May you always throw kindness around like confetti.

There once was a red chicken named Blue.
God blessed him with a boy and their friendship grew.

Blue and the boy had many adventures.

In the morning, they would watch the sunrise and listen for the rooster's crow.

Peck at blueberry waffles;
add so much syrup that the plate would overflow.

When breakfast had been eaten,
Blue perched on the boy's shoulder.
He touched the boy with his feathers.

"Cluck, chirp, cheep."

That's how he said "love" with a beak.

The boy, in turn, hugged Blue tight.

"Thump, thump, thump."

Blue felt love from the boy's heartbeat.

As afternoon sprung,
Oh, how Blue and his boy would run!

The two would sword fight,
stick versus beak,
ride through fields on a tractor,
skip rocks in the creek.

Before bed, Blue and his boy would watch the sunset.
Sitting on the porch, they cuddled neck to neck.

They thanked the Lord for each other
and then got comfy under their sheets.

Blue purred to the boy,

"Cluck, chirp, cheep."

That's how he said "love" with a beak.

The boy, in turn, hugged Blue tight.

"Thump, thump, thump."

Blue felt love from the boy's heartbeat.

One morning while sharing blueberry waffles,
Blue and his boy got into a scuffle.
The boy dipped it in syrup and started to eat the last piec
Instead of sharing, Blue bit the boy with his beak!

He was angry and did not say,
"Cluck, chirp, cheep."

The boy was hurt;
Blue did not hear
"thump, thump, thump"
from the boy's heartbeat.

When afternoon sprung,
the two didn't run.

There were no sword fights, stick versus beak.
They didn't ride tractors,
or skip rocks in the creek.

Before bed the two sat on the porch, but with a wide gap.
Blue slowly walked towards the boy and his wings softly flapped
He missed his friend and the fun they had.
Knowing he hurt the boy made Blue awfully sad.

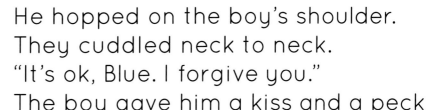

He hopped on the boy's shoulder.
They cuddled neck to neck.
"It's ok, Blue. I forgive you."
The boy gave him a kiss and a peck.

That night they headed inside
and got comfy under their sheets.

Blue purred to the boy,

"Cluck, chirp, cheep."

That's how he said "love" with a beak.

The boy, in turn, hugged Blue tight.

"Thump, thump, thump."

Blue felt love from the boy's heartbeat.

Photo credit: Captured by Katie

Jordan Nix - Author

Jordan Nix (left) resides in Lakeland, Tennessee with her husband, Josh, and two young sons. The author based this story off of her oldest son's imaginary chicken, Blue, who has been the accused culprit of many antics around their home. Nix received her bachelor's degree in journalism, as well as earned an English minor from the University of Memphis. She currently serves her community as a photographer and freelance writer.

Nicole Manes - Illustrator

Nicole Manes (right) currently resides in Memphis, Tennessee with her dog, Bear. The illustrator has a Bachelor of Fine Arts degree and a Master's of Information Visualization degree. Manes works full-time as a data analyst for ALSAC/St. Jude Children's Research Hospital. Additionally, the illustrator takes her artistic skillset to another level as the owner and operator of ANP Cakes.

Nix and Manes have been friends since they were third graders at St. Ann School. Their friendship spans 20+ years.